4.95

If You Were a Ballet Dancer

If You Were a Ballet Dancer

RUTH BELOV GROSS

The Dial Press   New York

Published by The Dial Press
1 Dag Hammarskjold Plaza
New York, New York 10017

My thanks to all the people who helped with this book—the ballet teachers who graciously allowed visits to their classes, the dancers and the students who answered endless questions, and the administrative personnel of ballet schools and ballet companies who smoothed the way. I am especially grateful to the School of American Ballet in New York City; to Leslie Bailey, press assistant of the New York City Ballet; and to David Richardson of the New York City Ballet.

Most of all I am indebted to the consultant for this book, Suki Schorer, who was formerly a principal dancer with the New York City Ballet and who is now a member of the faculty of the School of American Ballet.

R.B.G.

Manufactured in the United States of America / Second Dial Printing, 1981

Library of Congress Cataloging in Publication Data
Gross, Ruth Belov. If you were a ballet dancer.
Reprint of the ed. published by Scholastic Book Services, New York.
Summary: In question-and-answer format, Ruth Belov Gross discusses the life and career of ballet dancers.
I. Ballet—Vocational guidance—Juvenile literature.
[I. Ballet dancing] I. Title.
GV1787.5.G76 1980 792.8′023 79-3583
ISBN 0-8037-5383-7 ISBN 0-8037-5384-5 lib. bdg.

For Willy
with all my love

If you were a ballet dancer, you would dance on a stage.

There would be music, and you would dance to the music.
People would come to watch you dance.
You would spin around and around.
You would whirl and jump and leap.

The people would clap and cheer.
And you would feel happy.

The next morning you would get up early.
You would put on your practice clothes
and begin practicing.

If you were a ballet dancer,
you would practice every single day.

What is it like to be a ballet dancer?
Is ballet just for girls, or is it for boys too?
How do ballet dancers learn to do the things they do?
Now you can find out!

When should you begin to take ballet lessons?

A good time to begin taking ballet lessons is when you are eight or nine years old. Many famous ballet dancers started when they were a little older or a little younger, though.

These boys and girls are trying out for ballet school.

These students look more like ballet dancers. They have been studying for a year or two.

How long does it take to become a
ballet dancer?

It takes about eight or ten years of training.

At first, ballet students go to ballet school once or twice a week. When they are 11 or 12 years old, they go to ballet school every day.

When the students are about 15 years old, they begin to take 10 or 15 lessons a week. They spend most of their time taking ballet lessons.

Ballet students usually go to ballet school until they are 17 or 18 years old. Then, if they are good enough, they can begin their careers as dancers.

Do you have to go to regular school too while you are learning to be a ballet dancer?

Yes — and you also have to do your homework for regular school.

In some countries, students learn ballet and do their regular schoolwork all in the same school. They eat and sleep at school and only go home for visits.

Do you have homework for ballet classes?

No — at least not when you are beginning. If you practiced at home, you might make mistakes, and nobody would be there to help you do things right.

These ballet students are dancing in a ballet called *Coppélia*.

How old do you have to be to dance in a performance?

You can dance in a performance when you are 10 or 11 years old, or maybe even sooner. But you would still have to keep on going to ballet school until you are 17 or 18 years old.

In many ballet schools, the students give a performance every year, to show what they have learned. And sometimes ballet students get to dance in a performance with real ballet dancers, when there are parts for children.

Why does it take so long to become a ballet dancer?

Ballet dancing looks easy, but it isn't easy at all.

Ballet dancers must be able to spin around and around without getting dizzy.

They must be able to raise one leg very, very slowly, until their toes are higher than their ears.

They must be able to leap high in the air, and to kick frontwards, sideways, and backwards.

It takes a lot of training to do things like that. Boys also have to learn how to lift a girl into the air. And girls have to learn to dance on their toes.

Ballet dancers have to make lifting —
and everything else they do — look easy.

What is the first thing you learn in ballet school?

The very first thing you learn is how to stand like a dancer.

Ordinary people stand with their toes and their knees pointing straight ahead.

Ballet dancers learn to stand with their toes and their knees pointing out to the side.

If they did not turn their feet and legs out to the side, ballet dancers could not do their ballet steps properly.

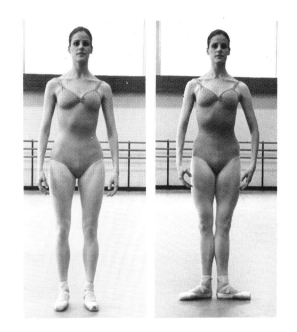

Ballet dancers start and finish their exercises and steps in one of these five positions.

First position

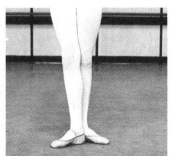

Second position

Third position

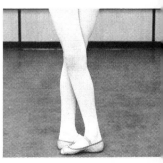

Fourth position

Fifth position

How do ballet dancers make up the steps they do?

They don't make up the steps. They learn them in ballet school. Most of the steps were made up 200 or 300 years ago.

Ballet dancers have to know how to do hundreds of steps.

One step that boys learn is called an *air turn*. Sometimes girls learn it too.

To do an air turn, you jump straight up in the air, turn all the way around while you are in the air, and then come down again.

Ballet students practice doing air turns
until they can do them without falling down.
That may take two or three years!

*When they are in a ballet, can dancers
do air turns any time they want to?*

No. They can't do the steps they feel like
doing. They have to do the steps that some-
body else — a person called a *choreographer*
(**core**-ee-**og**-raff-er) — wants them to do.

A choreographer makes up a ballet by
putting different steps together. The dancers
learn the ballet the way you learn a poem
or a song.

A ballet is music and dancing and scenery and costumes, all put together. In some ballets there is a story too — but the dancers do not talk. They can tell the story without using words.

In some ballets, there is no story. A ballet that does not tell
a story is like a beautiful design. The design keeps changing
as the dancers move to the music.

Where do ballet dancers practice?

Ballet dancers practice in a large room called a studio. Ballet students take their lessons there too.

Big mirrors in the studio help the dancers see what they are doing right and what they are doing wrong. Wooden bars along the walls help the dancers keep their balance.

Dancers usually have music when they dance. So there is always a piano or a record player or a tape recorder in a ballet studio. There is no other furniture.

*Do you wear special clothes for
ballet lessons?*

Yes. Regular clothes cover you up too
much, and the teacher can't see how you
move. You wear the same kind of practice
clothes that ballet dancers wear.

The boys usually wear tights and a T-shirt.
In some ballet schools they also wear long
white socks.

The girls usually wear tights and a leotard.
A leotard looks something like a bathing suit.
Sometimes the older girls also wear a little
skirt.

Girls have to pin their hair up, so it doesn't
get in their eyes when they bend or turn.

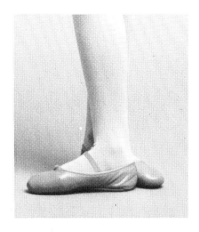

Soft ballet shoes have elastic straps to keep them from falling off.

Toe shoes are tied on with satin ribbons. Sometimes girls also have satin ribbons on their soft ballet shoes.

What kind of shoes do you wear?

When you begin taking ballet lessons, you wear soft ballet shoes. You can dance on tiptoe in these shoes, but not on the ends of your toes.

Boys do not learn to dance on the ends of their toes. Girls do, so later on girls wear special toe shoes part of the time.

Toe shoes are hard and stiff in front, and they are flat at the very tip. The flat part is what the dancer stands on when she is standing on the ends of her toes. The stiffness keeps her toes from bending.

When do girls learn to dance on their toes?

Girls can usually begin to wear toe shoes when they are 11 or 12 years old. They have to wait until their bones are hard enough and the muscles in their feet and legs are strong enough.

A dancer can't dance on the tips of her toes unless she is wearing toe shoes. Even then, she can't stay on just one foot very long. She would lose her balance after about four seconds. When she has a partner to help her, she can stay on her toes much longer.

Are girls better at ballet than boys?

No. It used to seem that way, though.

For a long time, all the famous ballet stars were women. The men did not have very much to do in a ballet.

Then choreographers began to put a lot of very hard steps in their ballets for men to do. Everybody could see what good dancers men really were. Now some of the most famous ballet stars in the world are men.

Men and boys are better at jumping and leaping than women and girls are. So in most ballets, the male dancers do a lot of difficult jumps and leaps.

Lifting is one of the hardest things to do in ballet. The
man has to be careful not to drop his partner, and she has to
be careful not to poke her elbow in his teeth. The dancers
have to practice together a lot to get everything right.

How do ballet dancers turn around and around without getting dizzy?

Ballet dancers have a little trick that keeps them from getting dizzy.

Before they turn, they pick something to look at — a doorway, maybe, or a clock on the wall. Then they try to keep looking at it while they are going around and around.

This works most of the time. Sometimes ballet dancers get dizzy anyway.

How can ballet dancers kick their legs so high?

Ballet dancers do special exercises to stretch their muscles. The more they stretch their muscles, the higher their legs can go. They also have to do exercises to make their muscles strong.

Ballet dancers begin stretching their muscles when they are very young.

What happens when you finish ballet school? Are you a real ballet dancer right away?

After you finish ballet school, you can become a *professional* ballet dancer. That means you would be paid for dancing, and you could earn your living as a ballet dancer.

Most professional ballet dancers belong to a ballet company. Belonging to a ballet company is something like belonging to a football team. The members of the company practice together and perform together, and they get a salary.

When you go to the ballet, you will see many good dancers — but only a few real stars.

When a girl belongs to a ballet company, is she called a ballerina?

No. Only the *very* best dancers are called ballerinas. A ballerina is a star. There is something special about her dancing.

Boys can become ballet stars too, but they are not called ballerinas. A male star is called a *premier danseur* (pruhm-yay don-**ser**). That's French for "first dancer."

*Do professional ballet dancers get paid
a lot of money?*

The only ballet dancers who make a lot of
money are the stars. A few famous ballet stars
earn more than a million dollars a year!

Most professional ballet dancers are not
rich at all. Some of them have to have extra
jobs, like baby-sitting, to get along.

*What do professional ballet dancers
do all day?*

They practice, practice, practice! Ballet
dancers practice from 10 or 11 o'clock in the
morning until it is almost time for them to
perform at night.

First the dancers take a ballet lesson. They
call it "taking class." They do special ballet
exercises in class, and they practice one ballet
step after another.

Then, for the rest of the day, they practice
for their performances.

Why do ballet dancers have to take lessons?

Professional ballet dancers have to stay in shape, just like professional athletes. Dancers get a good workout in class, and the exercises keep their muscles strong.

Ballet dancers also have another reason for taking class every day — they want to be better dancers. They know they can become better if they work very hard in class. Maybe that is why some of the very best dancers take two or three classes every day.

Every class begins at the bar. The dancers do the same things in class they did when they were children — but they do everything better now. The first exercise is a *plié* (plee-ay).

A teacher helps the dancers improve their dancing. "No matter how good you are," a famous dancer said, "you always need teaching."

Professional ballet dancers often wear their oldest, most raggedy practice clothes in class. They almost always wear sweaters and woolly leg warmers too, to help keep their muscles warm.

When class is over, the dancers are tired. They get hot and sweaty when they dance, so they need to have a towel handy. They keep their towels — and their leg warmers and their sweaters and some extra shoes — in a big bag.

Ballet dancers make sure they have plenty of rosin on their shoes, to keep from slipping. The rosin is in the box, and the dancers dip their shoes in it just before they dance.

Do ballet dancers ever hurt themselves?

Yes — very often. They hurt their backs and their shoulders and their necks and their knees. They pull their muscles, sprain their ankles, twist their joints, and break small bones in their feet. Sometimes a dancer even breaks a leg.

Ballet dancers do everything they can to keep from getting hurt. They do warm-up exercises before they dance, to loosen up their muscles. They put rosin powder on their shoes. That helps to keep them from slipping. And they try not to bump into each other.

Even so, there is always a chance that a dancer will get hurt.

Ballet dancers do warm-up exercises before every class, before
every rehearsal, and before every performance. Every ballet
dancer has a favorite way of warming up.

What happens when ballet dancers are tired or don't feel well?

They dance anyway. They dance when they are tired, they dance when they have colds, they dance with upset stomachs. Even when they sprain an ankle, they try to keep on dancing.

Most dancers say they don't feel any pain while they are dancing. They feel it later.

Do ballet dancers get nervous before a performance?

Some dancers never get nervous. Some feel scared before every performance. But when they begin to dance, even the nervous dancers stop feeling scared.

Dancers don't say good luck to each other before they go onstage. They think it's bad luck to say good luck — so they say "break a leg" or something like that. In one company the dancers say "chukkers" to each other. Nobody knows what it means.

It takes about two hours to get ready
for a performance. First the dancers
put on their make-up and their costumes,
and then they do warm-up exercises
for an hour or so. They need lots
of make-up so the audience can
see their faces from far away.
The men wear make-up too.

What do dancers do after a performance?

They eat! Ballet dancers can't eat a big meal before they dance, so they are very hungry afterward.

But first they take off their make-up and their costumes, take a shower, and put on their regular clothes.

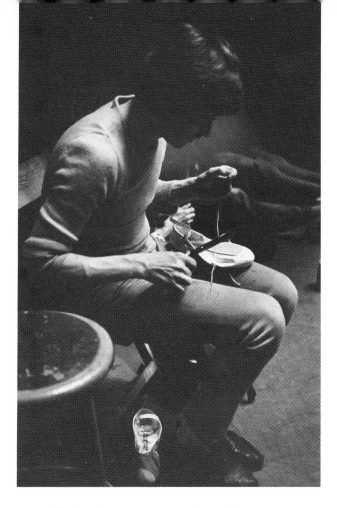

Ballet dancers spend a lot of time sewing the ribbons and elastic bands on their ballet shoes. The shoes do not come with ribbons and bands because every dancer wants them put on a different way.

What do dancers do on their day off?

They do all the things that everybody else does on their day off. They do the laundry, go to the supermarket, clean the house, see a movie, or wash the dog.

They also do some ballet exercises, sew ribbons on their ballet shoes, and maybe take a class.

What about sports?

Ballet dancers go swimming sometimes, because swimming is good for their muscles. But dancers are not supposed to do any sports that could hurt their bones or muscles.

If they played soccer, they might break a toe. If they went skating, they might twist an ankle. And they could break a leg if they went skiing. Then they couldn't dance.

Do dancers make their own costumes?

No, the costumes are made by special costume makers. Some ballet costumes cost more than a thousand dollars each.

A ballet costume has to fit right and look beautiful. And it has to be extra strong so it doesn't come apart when a dancer leaps around the stage in it.

A ballet company may use the same costumes over and over for 10 years or more. That is why dancers cannot keep their costumes. They can keep their shoes, though.

The dancer on the left is wearing a *tutu* (too-too) — and so is the dancer on the right. The short tutu is called a *classic* tutu. The long one is called a *romantic* tutu. There are many other kinds of ballet costumes. You can see some of them on the next page.

Queen from *The Sleeping Beauty*

Outlaw from *Billy the Kid*

Angels from *The Nutcracker*

Tin Soldier from *The Steadfast Tin Soldier*

How long do ballet shoes last?

Not very long — maybe only a couple of hours. Sometimes a dancer wears out two pairs of shoes in just one performance.

Most professional ballet dancers need nine or ten new pairs of shoes every week. Dancers who belong to a ballet company are lucky, because the company pays for the shoes.

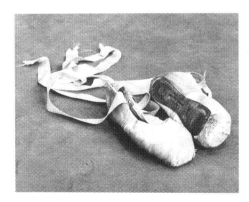

These toe shoes were worn for one performance. They can only be used for practicing now.

*Do children who take ballet lessons
always grow up to be ballet dancers?*

No. Some ballet students may not be good
enough to become professional ballet dancers
— or they decide they would rather do something else. But they will be more graceful
than they were before, and they are likely to
be better at sports.

Sometimes professional athletes take ballet
lessons because they know that ballet training
will help them improve their speed and
balance.

These are not dancers. They are football players.
They are taking ballet lessons to help them
play football better.

Can you get married and have children if you are a ballet dancer?

Some ballet dancers get married, and some do not. Very often, two ballet dancers fall in love and marry each other.

Sometimes the children of ballet dancers become dancers too.

When do dancers have to stop being dancers?

Most dancers stop dancing when they are about 35 or 40 years old — about the time professional athletes have to retire. Not many ballet dancers keep on dancing when they are more than 45 years old.

What do ballet dancers do when they can't dance anymore?

Some teach other dancers. Some become choreographers. Some run ballet companies.

Other dancers begin a whole new career. They may become writers or photographers — or they may even open a restaurant.

If ballet dancers have to retire early,
and if they work so hard
and don't get paid very much
and get badly hurt sometimes —
why do they dance?

Ballet dancers dance because they love dancing.

Some special ballet words

If you were a ballet dancer, you could go to almost any country in the world and take a ballet class. You would understand the teacher because ballet words are the same everywhere.

Ballet words are mostly French words. That's because the first ballet school — about 300 years ago — was in France. Ever since then, ballet dancers have been using the same special ballet words.

Here are some of them.

arabesque

arabesque (ah-ra-**besk**) — a ballet pose. In an *arabesque*, the dancer stands on one leg and stretches the other leg high in back. When the dancer leans far forward, as in this photograph, it is called an *arabesque penchée* (ah-ra-**besk** pon-**shay**).

ballerina (bal-uh-**ree**-nah) — a ballet star. *Ballerinas* are the very best female dancers in a ballet company. It takes talent and many years of hard work to become a *ballerina.*

barre (bahr) — the wooden bar that is fastened to the wall of a ballet studio. See the pictures on page 32. Dancers hold on to the bar for some of their exercises. It helps them keep their balance. Every ballet class begins at the *barre.*

corps de ballet (core duh ba-**lay**) — the dancers in a ballet company who dance together in a group. They are something like the singers in a chorus. The picture on page 6 shows a *corps de ballet.*

grand jeté (grahn zhuh-**tay**) — a big leap in the air. See the picture on page 7.

pas (pah) — a step in ballet.

pas de chat (**pah** duh **shah**) — cat step. *Chat* means cat in French, and the step is called *pas de chat* because it looks something like the way a cat would jump.

pas de deux (pah duh **duh**) — a dance for two people. A dance for three people is called a *pas de trois* (pah duh **twah**). *Trois* means three in French.

pirouette

pirouette (peer-oo-**wet**) — a turn in which the dancer spins around on one foot. A dancer must have very good balance to do one *pirouette* after another.

plié (plee-**ay**) — a special kind of knee bend that dancers do. Dancers do a *plié* at the beginning and end of every jump. The dancers in the photographs on page 32 are practicing *pliés*.

pointes (pwant) — the tips of the toes. When a dancer is on the tips of her toes, we say that she is on *pointe*. She must wear special toe shoes to dance this way. See page 24.

premier danseur (pruhm-**yay** don-**ser**) — a male ballet star. A *premier danseur* often does a *pas de deux* with a *ballerina*.

révérence

révérence (ray-vay-**rahnce**) — a deep bow, the kind dancers make to the audience at the end of a ballet. In many ballet schools, the students end each class with a *révérence*.

tour en l'air (toor ahn lair) — also called *air turn* — a complete turn that a dancer makes in the air. See page 18.

tutu (too-too) — the fluffy skirt that is worn in many ballets. Some *tutus* are short, and some are long. See the photographs on page 39.

photo credits

Steven Caras, front cover, Patricia McBride and Bart Cook in *Sonatine*, New York City Ballet; back cover, Nina Fedorova in *Coppélia*, New York City Ballet; 17 bottom, 28, School of American Ballet; 32 right, Ballet Nacional de Cuba; 35, American Ballet Theatre; 39 left, Marie Calegari, New York City Ballet; 41 left, Mikhail Baryshnikov in *The Steadfast Tin Soldier*, New York City Ballet; 41 right. **Susan Cook** for Capezio Ballet Makers, 24 bottom. **Costas,** 27, Melinda Roy & Christopher d'Amboise in *Dances at a Gathering* performed by the School of American Ballet. **Kenn Duncan,** 39 right, Jolinda Menendez, American Ballet Theatre; 40 top left, Sallie Wilson in *The Sleeping Beauty*, American Ballet Theatre. **Maren and Reed Erskine,** 2, 8, 11, 13, School of American Ballet; 14, Heather Watts in *Coppélia*, New York City Ballet, with students from the School of American Ballet; 17 top, Merrill Ashley, New York City Ballet; 34, Suzanne Farrell and Marjorie Spohn, New York City Ballet; 37, Heather Watts, New York City Ballet; 38. **Lois Greenfield,** 10, Public School #1, Chinatown, New York City; 16 right, Mikhail Baryshnikov & Christine Sarry in *Variations on America*, The Feld Ballet; 21, *Kammermusik #2*, New York City Ballet; 24 top, for Capezio Ballet Makers; 30, Gelsey Kirkland & Mikhail Baryshnikov in *Theme and Variations*, American Ballet Theatre; 33 top left, Dance Theatre of Harlem. **Paul Kolnik,** 7, Merrill Ashley in *The Nutcracker*, New York City Ballet; 23, School of American Ballet; 33 top right, New York City Ballet; 33 bottom, Lyric Opera of Chicago Ballet. **Delia Peters,** 18 and 32 left, School of American Ballet; 47, Patricia McBride, New York City Ballet. **Martha Swope,** 6, *The Nutcracker*, New York City Ballet; 15 top, Merrill Ashley, New York City Ballet; 15 bottom, Mikhail Baryshnikov in *Coppélia*, New York City Ballet; 20, Rebecca Wright & Greg Osborne in *The Nutcracker*, American Ballet Theatre; 26 left, Fernando Bujones in *Le Corsaire*, American Ballet Theatre; 26 right, Mikhail Baryshnikov and Marianna Tcherkassky in *Le Spectre de la Rose*, American Ballet Theatre; 40 top right, Terry Orr in *Billy the Kid*, American Ballet Theatre; 45, Marianna Tcherkassky & Ivan Nagy in *Giselle*, American Ballet Theatre; 46, Merrill Ashley, New York City Ballet. **Jay Thompson,** 16 left, Rancho High School, North Las Vegas, Nevada. **Joel Weltman,** 40 bottom right, students from the School of American Ballet in *The Nutcracker*, New York City Ballet. **Wide World,** 42. **Rosemary Winckley,** 25, Mikhail Baryshnikov & Natalia Makarova in *Don Quixote*, American Ballet Theatre. **WNET/13 New York,** back cover, students from the School of American Ballet.